# ALBERT DOUBLES THE FUN

by **Eleanor May** • Illustrated by **Deborah Melmon**

THE KANE PRESS / NEW YORK

Acknowledgments: We wish to thank the following people for their helpful advice and review of the material contained in this book: Susan Longo, Former Early Childhood and Elementary School Teacher, Mamaroneck, NY; and Rebeka Eston Salemi, Kindergarten Teacher, Lincoln School, Lincoln, MA.

Special thanks to Susan Longo for providing the Fun Activities in the back of this book.

Library of Congress Cataloging-in-Publication Data

Names: May, Eleanor, author. | Melmon, Deborah, illustrator.
Title: Albert doubles the fun / by Eleanor May ; illustrated by Deborah Melmon.
Description: New York : The Kane Press, 2017. | Series: Mouse math | Summary: At the fair Albert the mouse demonstrates doubling numbers from one to ten.
Identifiers: LCCN 2015030607 (print) | LCCN 2015051458 (ebook) | ISBN 9781575658346 (reinforced library binding : alk. paper) | ISBN 9781575658353 (pbk. : alk. paper) | ISBN 9781575658360 (pdf)
Subjects: | CYAC: Fairs—Fiction. | Addition—Fiction. | Mice—Fiction.
Classification: LCC PZ7.M4513 Aj 2016 (print) | LCC PZ7.M4513 (ebook) | DDC [E]—dc23
LC record available at https://lccn.loc.gov/2015030607

1 3 5 7 9 10 8 6 4 2

First published in the United States of America in 2017 by Kane Press, Inc.
Printed in China

Book Design: Edward Miller

Mouse Math is a registered trademark of Kane Press, Inc.

Visit us online at **www.kanepress.com**

 Like us on Facebook
facebook.com/kanepress

 Follow us on Twitter
@KanePress

Dear Parent/Educator,

"I can't do math." Every child (or grownup!) who says these words has at some point along the way felt intimidated by math. For young children who are just being introduced to the subject, we wanted to create a world in which math was not simply numbers on a page, but a part of life—an adventure!

Enter Albert and Wanda, two little mice who live in the walls of a People House. Children will be swept along with this irrepressible duo and their merry band of friends as they tackle mouse-sized problems and dilemmas (and sometimes *cat-sized* problems and dilemmas!).

Each book in the **MOUSE MATH**® series provides a fresh take on a basic math concept. The mice discover solutions as they, for instance, use position words while teaching a pet snail to do tricks or count the alarmingly large number of friends they've invited over on a rainy day—and, lo and behold, they are doing math!

Math educators who specialize in early childhood learning have applied their expertise to make sure each title is as helpful as possible to young children—and to their parents and teachers. Fun activities at the ends of the books and on our website encourage kids to think and talk about math in ways that will make each concept clear and memorable.

As with our award-winning Math Matters® series, our aim is to captivate children's imaginations by drawing them into the story, and so into the math at the heart of each adventure. It is our hope that kids will want to hear and read the **MOUSE MATH** stories again and again and that, as they grow up, they will approach math with enthusiasm and see it as an invaluable tool for navigating the world they live in.

Sincerely,

*Joanne Kane*

Joanne E. Kane
Publisher

**MOUSE MATH titles:**

**Albert Adds Up!**
Adding/Taking Away

**Albert Doubles the Fun**
Adding Doubles

**Albert Helps Out**
Counting Money

**Albert Is NOT Scared**
Direction Words

**Albert Keeps Score**
Comparing Numbers

**Albert's Amazing Snail**
Position Words

**Albert's BIGGER Than Big Idea**
Comparing Sizes: Big/Small

**Albert Starts School**
Days of the Week

**Albert the Muffin-Maker**
Ordinal Numbers

**A Beach for Albert**
Capacity

**Bravo, Albert!**
Patterns

**Count Off, Squeak Scouts!**
Number Sequence

**If the Shoe Fits**
Nonstandard Units of Measurement

**Lost in the Mouseum**
Left/Right

**Make a Wish, Albert!**
3D Shapes

**Mice on Ice**
2D Shapes

**The Mousier the Merrier!**
Counting

**A Mousy Mess**
Sorting

**The Right Place for Albert**
One-to-One Correspondence

**Where's Albert?**
Counting & Skip Counting

At breakfast, Albert couldn't eat a crumb.
His sister, Wanda, was going to take him to the fair!

"Can Leo come?" he asked. Leo was his best friend.

Wanda smiled. "Why not? Maybe Lucy can come, too."

CRUMBS

But Leo and Lucy weren't home.

"Leo will miss all the fun," Albert said.
Then he brightened. "I'll just have to have fun for both
of us. Double the fun!"

At the fair, the mouse at the gate handed Wanda a map. Albert took one, too.

"One map for us, and one to bring to Leo," he explained.

"Good idea!" Wanda said. "Now where should we go first?"

 MAP MOUSE COUNTY FAIR   MAP MOUSE COUNTY FAIR

$1 + 1 = 2$

"Look!" Albert pointed.

It was their gym teacher, Mr. Mousely, in a dunking booth.

When Albert hit the target, Mr. Mousely fell into the water.

Albert bought another ticket.

"Sorry, Mr. Mousely!" he called out.
"Since Leo isn't here, I have to double dunk!"

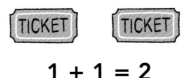

**1 + 1 = 2**

Wanda and Albert rode the Ferris wheel . . .

twice.

"Let's go again!" Albert said.

Wanda said, "But we already went two times."

"That was for me," Albert explained.
"Now I have to go twice for Leo, too."

**2 + 2 = 4**

After their fourth ride, Wanda wobbled away from the Ferris wheel.

"Let's go see the cheese sculptures," she said. "I'd like to look at something that stands still!"

They went into the big tent.
While Wanda checked out the cheese sculptures,
Albert eyed the cakes and pies.

Judges' Table

"Hungry?" a mouse asked. "The pie eating contest
is about to start!"

Albert slid into the last empty seat.
The judge set a slice of pie in front of him and tied a
bib around his neck.

"Remember," the judge said. "No paws allowed!"

"Ready . . . set . . . nibble!"

Albert quickly ate three slices.

"Don't you think that's enough?" Wanda asked.

"Enough for me," Albert agreed.
"But I need to eat three for Leo, too!"

**3 + 3 = 6**

The judge pinned a blue ribbon to Albert's shirt.

"Leo and I can share the ribbon," Albert said. "Since I ate double the pie for him."

Wanda shook her head. "I just hope you don't get a double bellyache!"

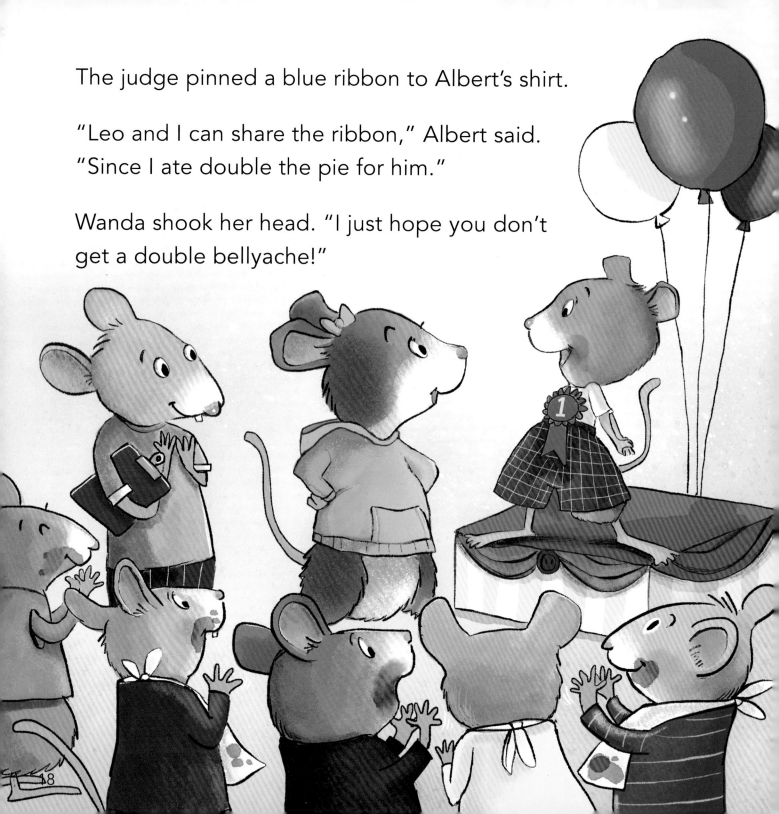

18

For once, Albert passed by the mice cream pops.

But at the ring toss, he stopped short.

"Scamper right up and win a prize!" the mouse behind the counter said.

"Look, Wanda!" Albert squeaked. "Robo-Rat action figures! Only four prize tokens for the whole set!"

It took Albert a long time to win a prize token.

"With one token, you can get a candle that looks
like a piece of cheese," Wanda said.

Albert shook his head. "I want the Robo-Rats."

21

When Albert won a second token, Wanda suggested, "You could get a giant bumblebee."

Albert said, "Robo-Rats."

When Albert won his third token, Wanda didn't say anything.

"I won four tokens!" Albert yelled. "Now I can get the Robo-Rats!"

Wanda said, "Great! Let's go!"

"We can't go yet," Albert said. "I still need to win four more tokens."

4 + 4 = 8

"Four MORE?" Wanda asked.

Albert nodded. "So I can get Leo a set of action figures, too!"

The mouse behind the counter rested his chin on his paw. "Scamper right up," he said glumly.

Albert did.

"Five action figures in each set! Five for me, and five for Leo," Albert said. "I can't wait to see his face!"

Wanda pointed. "Albert, isn't that—"

**5 + 5 = 10**

"LEO!" Albert said. "We wanted to take you to the fair with us, but you weren't home!"

Leo grinned. "That's because I was at the fair!"

"Look what I got you!" Albert said.

Leo said, "Look what I got YOU!"

"Now we have twenty action figures," Albert said.

"That's a lot," Leo agreed. "More than we need."

**10 + 10 = 20**

"We could give some to our sisters," Albert said.

"No, thank you," Wanda said. "I don't like robots."

"I don't like RATS!" Lucy said.

Then Albert said, "I have an idea. . . ."

A crowd of mice gathered around Albert and Leo's ring toss.

"Scamper right up and win a prize!" Leo called out.

"Or two prizes!" Albert said. "One for you, one for a friend . . . double the fun!"

*Albert Doubles the Fun* supports children's understanding of **adding doubles**, an important topic in early math learning. Use the activities below to extend the math topic and to support children's early reading skills.

## 🐭 ENGAGE

▶ Begin by holding up the cover and asking the children what they think this story may be about. (You may want to cover the title so that it's not a giveaway!) Record their predictions and refer back to them at the end of the story.

▶ Uncover the title and read it aloud. Ask the children if any of them have ever been to a fair or a carnival. What are some of their favorite rides and games? What are other fun activities to do at the fair? Encourage children to share their stories.

▶ Tell children that it's time to read the story and find out how Albert "doubles the fun"!

## 🐭 LOOK BACK

▶ After reading the story, ask the children if they can retell it in their own words. What happens in the beginning of the story, in the middle, and at the end?

▶ Ask the children why they think Albert wanted to double the number of prizes he won. How was he able to do this?

▶ Ask: *Who can describe how Wanda felt about Albert doubling everything throughout the story?* Ask the children to find parts of the story that back up their responses (they may use words or illustrations from the story to make their points).

▶ At the end of the story, why did Albert and Leo have so many action figures? How did this happen? What did they decide to do with all the extra ones?

▶ Encourage children to think about what they would have done with all the extra toys. How would they change the ending of the story? Record their ideas. Then have children draw pictures that describe their new endings.

## 🐭 TRY THIS!

**Doubling Fun!**

▶ You'll need grid paper, dice, and crayons or markers for each child.

▶ Give each child a sheet of grid paper divided into six columns; each column should have one of these doubled numbers at the bottom: 2, 4, 6, 8, 10, 12.

▶ Distribute a die to each child, and give them these instructions: (1) roll the die and double the number that comes up; (2) find the new number at the bottom of your grid sheet; (3) color in the square above it.

▶ Have the children continue to roll their dice and practice doubling the numbers, coloring in one square at a time from the bottom and moving up. Tell them to raise their hands when they reach the top of a column. Give children about 10 minutes to practice doubling this way.

**Bonus!** Double the fun with partners! Pair up the children and give each child a fresh recording sheet. Children will take turns rolling the die and recording their doubled number on their own sheet until they reach the top of a column. Encourage children to double-check each other's work. The child who reaches the top of any column first is the winner! Children may continue to play, as time allows, to see which doubled number will reach the top next.

## 🐭 THINK!

▶ Have children work in pairs. Give each pair a deck of cards containing the numbers 1–10.

▶ Have each pair place the deck of cards face down between them. Explain that they will take turns picking up the top card and doubling that number. If a player correctly doubles the number, they keep that card. If the player is incorrect, they must give the card to their partner. The game continues until all the cards from the pile are gone.

▶ Tell the children to count the number of cards they have accumulated in their doubled number pile. The winner is the player with the most cards. If there's a tie, you may want to introduce the number cards 11–20 to make the next round a bit more challenging!

◆ **FOR MORE ACTIVITIES** ◆

**visit www.kanepress.com/mouse-math-activities**